RICKY VARGAS:

The Funniest Kid in the World

W9-BYE-202

For Mildred Feinsilver, the funniest teacher in the world.
—A. K.

For the funny Francis family, thanks for the laughs!
—S. C.

If you purchased this book without a cover, you should be aware that this book is stolen property. It was reported as "unsold and destroyed" to the publisher, and neither the author nor the publisher has received any payment for this "stripped book."

No part of this publication may be reproduced, stored in a retrieval system, or transmitted in any form or by any means, electronic, mechanical, photocopying, recording, or otherwise, without written permission of the publisher. For information regarding permission, write to Scholastic Inc., Attention: Permissions Department, 557 Broadway, New York, NY 10012.

Text copyright © 2010 by Alan Katz.
Illustrations copyright © 2010 by Scholastic Inc.

Illustrations by Stacy Curtis.
All rights reserved. Published by Scholastic Inc.
SCHOLASTIC, LITTLE APPLE, and associated logos are trademarks and/or registered trademarks of Scholastic Inc.

Library of Congress Cataloging-in-Publication Data is available.

ISBN 978-0-545-24583-8

10 9 8 7 6 5   21 22 23 24

Printed in the U.S.A. 40
First school market edition, October 2010

RICKY VARGAS:
The Funniest Kid in the World

Egg-stra funny!

by Alan Katz

with illustrations by Stacy Curtis

Scholastic Inc.

New York   Toronto   London   Auckland   Sydney   Mexico City   New Delhi   Hong Kong

Table of Contents

The Spelling Bee Story

Ricky Vargas is seven.

He is in second grade.

And he is funny.

Very funny.

Very, very, very funny.

So funny, he makes people
snort milk out of their noses.

Even when they're not
drinking milk.

Now *that's* funny.

Ricky is funny in the school yard....

Could someone please go look for me in the lost and found?!

Ricky is funny in class...

...like when his teacher
asked Ricky if he had a note from
his mother.

Ricky said, "Yes, Mrs. Wilder, I do!"

Then he took a deep breath and sang...
"Laaaaaaa..."

"That's a fine note." Mrs. Wilder
smiled. "But not the one I want."

"Okay, how about *this* one?" Ricky asked.

"Faaaaaaaaa..."

Ricky is funny in gym....

I told you to put on gym clothes.

At home, Ricky always finds
ways to crack up the family....

Ricky is even funny at
the doctor's office....

"Hello, Dr. Nelson," Ricky said.

He opened his mouth.

Then he stuck out his tongue
as far as it would go.

People always think
Ricky is a riot.

Of course, there are times
that Ricky gets so busy making
everyone laugh, he loses track of
what he really should be
doing.

That happened last week—
at the Spelling Bee....

Ricky's pal Eddie had scored by spelling TOWEL, so their class was only one point behind. It was Ricky's turn, and he knew it was a big moment.

Everyone was quiet.

Miss Young said, "Ricky, your
word is FOR—"

Ricky jumped right in.

He said, "Well, there's F-O-R,
as in, 'a gift *for* me!'
F-O-U-R, that's the number four.

There's F-O-R-E like in golf!
Fore!

"Wow, what a great shot!
Ricky Vargas gets a hole in one!
O-N-E!
And he won! W-O-N!"

"There's also T-W-O, T-O, and T-O-O!
Plus E-I-G-H-T, which is one more
than seven.
Also A-T-E like I *ate* a pie...."

Ricky went on for a long time.
A *really* long time.

At first, his teammates were laughing. But it wasn't so funny when Miss Young said...

Ricky froze.

His whole team froze.

Miss Young said, "Zero points!"

Because Ricky's spelling word wasn't FOR.

It was...FORGOT.

Ricky had gone too far.

And because of him,
his team lost.

L-O-S-T.

No one laughed at Ricky
the rest of the day.

TODAY'S FRENCH WORDS:

HAT = CHAPEAU

GIVE = DONNER

DOG = CHIEN

Well, maybe they did...*a little*.

You see, Ricky Vargas knows
what to do when he's made
a mistake.

And after all, he *is* the funniest kid
in the world.

The Class Picture Story

"Good morning, class,"
said Mrs. Wilder on a very, very, very, very
rainy day.

"I am glad everyone made it
to school on this very, very,
very rainy day," she added.

"You forgot one *very*," said
Ricky, pointing to the words
above her head.

"Yes, Ricky, it is a very, very, very, *very* rainy day indeed." Mrs. Wilder smiled. "It is a good day to stay inside!"

"Unless you're a tree!" Ricky said. "Or a llama. Or a moose."

Mrs. Wilder and the whole class
giggled.

They giggled even more
when Mrs. Wilder told Ricky he
was correct, and said, "If there
are any trees, llamas, or moose
in this classroom, please go back
outside right now!"

Mrs. Wilder added, "I am glad it's raining. That means we'll have inside recess, and you won't get messy or dirty on this very special day...."

"Does anyone know why today is so special?"

"No, Ricky...it's Class Picture
Day," the teacher said.
"So practice your very best
smiles for the camera."

And that's just what they did.

For a long time.

A *long* time.

Then the class had its
usual day of math and science
and reading and French lessons.

Mrs. Wilder kept telling the
students to stay neat and clean
for the pictures.

HA!
HA!
HA!

HA!
HA!

HA!

But at recess, Eddie got a bump
on his forehead when he
tried to knock down all the pins
by sliding into them....

Ricky helped him up and said,
"Eddie, you just got a spare.
Too bad you don't have
a spare *head*!"

At lunch, Kiera spilled a whole
cup of blueberry yogurt
on her new red-and-white sweater.

By the end of the day, Eddie's
bump was better and Mrs. Wilder
had carefully helped Kiera
turn her sweater around so the
yogurt wouldn't be seen.

Everyone lined up in the gym for the class picture.

"Okay, I want big smiles," said Miss Verdi, who was taking the pictures for the school.

"Everybody say, 'No homework!'" Ricky told the group.

"Nice try, Ricky," Mrs. Wilder said.
But saying 'Cheese' will be just fine."

"One...

...two..."

"CHEESE!"

A few days later, the class pictures came. Everyone was very, very, very, very excited! No one could tell Eddie had a bump. No one could tell Kiera was wearing a cup of yogurt on the back of her sweater.

But *everyone* could see Ricky trying to
make a funny face—but at the worst
possible time. Which didn't make
anyone laugh.

WILDER'S CLASS
:COND GRADE

44

Ricky said, "I'm sorry"
either 214 or 215 times.
(Eddie counted, and he wasn't sure
if number 108 was an "I'm sorry"
or a sneeze.)

But Ricky knew he had to do more.

That night, Ricky used the
family computer and found a
nice, smiling picture of himself.
He printed 22 copies on sticker paper,
cut them out, and brought them
to school the next day.

It was a perfect fit! Now everyone's class picture had a good shot of Ricky.

And Ricky learned an important lesson: It's okay to make funny faces on "one" and "two..."

But **never** on CHEESE!

How to Be the Funniest Kid in the World

Tongue Twisters

Ricky's pop playfully popped his perfect bubble.
Ricky pouted, then popped his pop's.

During lunches,
Ricky crunches.
Sips fruit punches
while he munches!

No joking, no jesting, no talking when testing!

Ricky's marvelous mutt took his mother's just-made muffins.

Ricky skillfully skates on safe city sidewalks.

Ricky, how do you spell 'rhythm'?

Wrong every time!

Ricky, can you tell me what comes after 99?

402

402 doesn't come after 99!

It does if you wait long enough!

How to Draw Ricky Vargas
by Stacy Curtis

"I may make this look easy, but it's hard being me." Try drawing Ricky for yourself.

Step #1
I start with his pudgy little nose.

Step #2
Then I draw his round eyes, a bit apart. I want Ricky to look happy, so let's add arching eyebrows.

Step #3
Next up is his face. Ricky has a slightly pointed chin and his ears are drawn in line with his eyes.

Step #4

Since Ricky is happy, draw him a smiling mouth! Add two simple lines for his shoulders.

Step #5

Finish with his hair and TA-DA! You've got Ricky Vargas!

For this game, all you need are a piece of paper and a pencil. On the paper, draw ten rows of ten dots so that it looks like a dotted square.

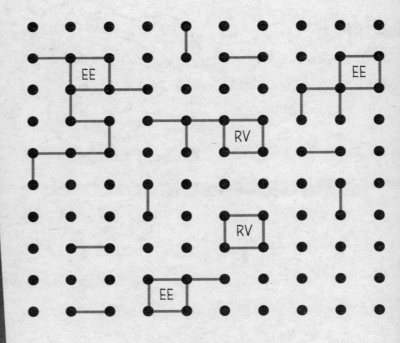

Each player takes turns drawing either a horizontal or a vertical line between a pair of dots. The dots must be next to each other, but can be anywhere in the square.

The goal of the game is to connect any four dots so they make a small box. Each time you create a box, write your initials in it. When the board is full, whoever creates the most boxes wins!